"META-GIRL: ORIGIN"

ART: JETHRO MORALES **COLORS:** EMMANUEL ORDAZ TORRES **LETTERS:** JAYMES REED

"HANNAH'S STORY"

ART: JETHRO MORALES **COLORS:** SANJU NIVANGUNE **LETTERS:** JON DEL ARROZ

"META-GIRL VS. DYNAMITE THOR"

ART: MARIAN MARS **COLORS:** EMMANUEL ORDAZ TORRES **LETTERS:** JON DEL ARROZ

CHARACTER BIOS

ART: JETHRO MORALES **COLORS:** LEVY RAMIREZ **LETTERS:** JAYMES REED

FLYING SPARKS

ALL STORIES BY JON DEL ARROZ

META-GIRL ORIGIN
HOW DOES THIS WORK AGAIN?
THESE ARE ANTI-GRAVITY ELLIPSES. THEY FIT WITHIN YOUR BOOTS AND INTERACT WITH YOUR BRAINWAVES SIMILARLY TO HOW YOU'RE ABLE TO WIGGLE YOUR TOES.
WHIRRR
IF THIS EXPERIMENT IS SUCCESSFUL, WE MIGHT BE ABLE TO CHANGE HOW PEOPLE TRAVEL.
SO, I THINK FLYING AND THEN IT HAPPENS?
THAT'S THE IDEA.
C'MON... FLY.

NOTHING HAPPENED.
LET ME CHECK--
IT'S WORKING!
HOW DO I GET IT TO *STOP* WORKING?!
WHOOSH!

WHAT IF I **CAN'T** STOP?
WHAT IF I KEEP GOING UP **FOREVER?**
I'M ONLY A **SOPHOMORE!**

PROFESSOR... HELP!
THUK!
CRAK!
OH, NO! THE SHARDS ARE GOING TO FALL ON SOMEONE.
HEY! WATCH OUT!

I'M THE ONLY ONE WHO CAN HELP.
THE ANT-GRAVITY ELLIPSES. I HAVE TO CONCENTRATE.

WHOOOOOOM!!!
I MADE IT!
ARE YOU OKAY?
I THINK SO, THANKS TO YOU.
I COULD HAVE DIED UP THERE.
I WAS VERY CONCERNED ABOUT YOUR SAFETY. BUT YOU'RE OKAY NOW. WE CAN STOP THE EXPERIMENTS IF YOU DON'T FEEL COMFORTABLE.
NO. I'VE NEVER FELT A RUSH LIKE THAT. LET'S KEEP IT GOING. WHO KNOWS WHAT COULD HAPPEN? IT MIGHT BE SOMETHING GOOD.
The Beginning

IT'S TOUGH BEING RICH.
BEFORE YOU ROLL YOUR EYES, I'VE HEARD IT ALL BEFORE.
"I'D JUST KILL TO HAVE YOUR LIFE."
"I'D BE SO HAPPY TO BE YOU!"
BRIIING
RIGHT.
IT'S SOOOO AWESOME TO BE UNABLE TO RELATE TO ANYONE.

I'M SMART ENOUGH TO GET BY WITHOUT MUCH STUDYING.
SO I SPEND MOST OF MY TIME DOING ONE OF THREE THINGS.
ONE: SHOPPING.
TWO: CLUBBING.
BABY YOU GOT SOME *MOVES!*
THREE: DATES WITH LAME GUYS.
AS YOU KNOW, I'M AN INVESTMENT BANKER, AND BANKERS MAKE MONEY LIKE--
THAT'S GREAT, MY BEST FRIEND'S A SUPERHERO.
HAHA, WOW, YOU'RE SO FUNNY.
PUH-LEEZE.
WOULD IT BE SO MUCH TO ASK TO MEET SOMEONE *INTERESTING* FOR A CHANGE?

"CAN I AT LEAST WALK YOU HOME?"
WHAT A TOOL.
MAIL
GIVE ME THE PURSE AND PUT YOUR HANDS IN THE AIR.
I NEED TO BE MORE CAREFUL WHAT I ASK FOR.
OH MY GOD, DON'T **SHOOT!**
I'LL DO **WHATEVER** YOU SAY!
SOMETIMES I WISH I HAD MY ROOMMATE CHLOE'S CONFIDENCE.
SHE WOULDN'T HAVE FROZEN WHILE HE GOT AWAY.
I MEAN, THAT WAS A **CHANEL** BAG!
DO YOU HAVE ANY IDEA HOW EXPENSIVE THOSE ARE?

THE POLICE ARRIVED LESS THAN AN HOUR AFTER THE INCIDENT.
AND THE DETECTIVE ASSIGNED TO THE CASE WAS REALLY ON TOP OF THINGS, BUT MOST IMPORTANTLY..
...HE WAS THE HOTTEST MAN I HAD EVER SEEN.
APPARENTLY, THE GUY I DESCRIBED WASN'T HARD TO FIND AT ALL.
THESE ARE THE REAL DEAL, GIRL.
GOT MILK?
THEY CAUGHT THAT $!&#* REALLY QUICK.
THANK YOU, THANK YOU FOR SAVING MY LIFE!
YOU MEAN GETTING YOUR PURSE BACK?
HOT AND EFFECTIVE, MY KIND OF GUY.

NATURALLY, THE FIRST THING I DID WAS FIND MY ROOMMATE AND TELL HER ALL ABOUT IT.
HE'S SOOOO CUTE.
AND WE TOTALLY HAVE THIS CHEMISTRY.
YOU COULD TELL WHEN I HUGGED HIM JUST BY THE WAY HIS BODY REACTED, ***SO TENSE.***
SO I THINK WE SHOULD CHANGE OUR ROUTE TO SCHOOL TO GO BY THE POLICE STATION.
IT'S REALLY NOT TOO FAR OUT OF OUR WAY.
NO WAY.
THAT'S GOING TO ADD AN EXTRA TEN MINUTES FOR SOME GUY YOU ***BARELY*** KNOW!
PLEEEAASSSE?
MY SUPER-ABILITY, THE ***CHARM ATTACK.***
NEVER FAILS.
...
I SWEAR, HANNAH, THIS IS THE ***LAST*** TIME.

MOST GUYS DON'T KNOW WHAT THEY WANT, SO YOU HAVE TO SHOW THEM.
TO SERVE AND PROTECT
IT'S NOT STALKING, IT'S BEING AGGRESSIVE.
!?
IT'S LIKE HE DIDN'T EVEN RECOGNIZE ME.
HE PROBABLY DIDN'T.
GRIP
WELL, HE WILL!
ALL RIGHT, SO I DON'T ALWAYS HAVE A WITTY RESPONSE.

SOMETIMES, YOU HAVE TO BE A LITTLE MORE AGGRESSIVE THAN OTHERS.
CAN I GO TO CLASS NOW?
SOMETIMES, YOU HAVE TO PULL OUT THE STOPS.
YOU LOOK RIDICULOUS.
IT'S NOT RIGHT.
WHY IS HE IGNORING ME?!
YOU KNOW, I THINK IT'S ILLEGAL FOR A COP TO GO AFTER A VICTIM OF A CRIME.
WHY DIDN'T YOU TELL ME THAT BEFORE I DRESSED LIKE THIS?!
YOU DIDN'T ASK.
SOMETIMES, NO MATTER WHAT YOU DO, YOU LOSE.

THAT'S ME IN A NUTSHELL.
RICH.
PRETTY.
POPULAR.
ALONE.
ON THE BRIGHT SIDE, OUR NEW ROUTE TO SCHOOL PASSED BY A PRETTY COOL NEW PLACE TO HANG OUT.
JOHNNY BEANS
WHO KNOWS, MAYBE I CAN FIND SOMEONE WHO CONNECTS WITH ME THERE?
HOW CAN I HELP YOU, MISS?
JACKPOT.

DYNAMITE THOR
A FORMER MINE OWNER WHO USES HIS EXPERT KNOWLEDGE OF HIGH EXPLOSIVES TO RID THE WORLD OF CRIME. IMMUNE TO THE EFFECTS OF EXPLOSIVES, HE CAN PROPEL HIMSELF THROUGH THE AIR WITH DYNAMITE!
YOU STUPID PRICK, THINK YOU CAN-
TREACHEROUS VILLAIN!
YOU ARE NO MATCH FOR DYNAMITE THOR!
OH MY!
KRAKOOM
CRUMBLE
FOOM
WOOPS...
A VICTORY FOR-
HOLD IT, SPEEDO-MAN.

FRIEND OR FOE?
META-GIRL
A TEACHER'S AIDE TO A BRILLIANT PHYSICIST, BENEFITING FROM HIS TECHNOLOGICAL CREATIONS TAKING UP THE MANTLE TO PROTECT THOSE OVERLOOKED BY MORE POWERFUL HEROES.
YE OLDE ENGLISH MUCH?
LET'S SAY I'M A CONCERNED CITIZEN.
CONCERNED? WHY?
ASKS THE MAN PROPELLING HIMSELF THROUGH THE AIR WITH EXPLOSIVES.
WELL, WHERE THERE'S CRIME THAT NEEDS FIGHTING, DYNAMITE THOR WILL BE THERE!
YOU SERIOUSLY CALL YOURSELF THAT?
HEY, WAIT UP...
MY APOLOGIES, I'M NOT USED TO WORKING WITH A PARTNER.
PARTNER?
YIKES! WATCH WHERE YOU THROW THAT STUFF!
LOOK! GANG VIOLENCE!

I'LL USE MY EXPERTISE OF EXPLOSIVES, AND THOSE FOOLS WILL NEVER SEE IT COMING!
STOP!
WHAT ARE YOU DOING?
YOU CAN'T JUST BLOW ALL YOUR PROBLEMS UP!
MISS, THAT'S WHAT I DO!
YOU WANTED TO TEAM UP, SO WE DO IT MY WAY. NO KILLING.
FINE.
LAY DOWN YOUR WEAPONS, EVILDOERS!
UGH... WHY CAN'T I MEET NORMAL PEOPLE DOING THIS?

DYNAMITE, TAKE THE ONE IN THE CAR, I'VE GOT THE OTHERS.
WHERE DO YOU THINK YOU'RE GOING?
BZZZT
BLAM
EAT DYNAMITE, SCUM!
BLAM BLAM
DYNAMITE THOR, NO!

KROOM!
THUD
THIS WAS A HUGE MISTAKE.
HAH!
MERE GANGSTERS ARE NO MATCH FOR THE MIGHTY POWER OF EXPLOSIVES!
VILLAINY DEFEATED!

SEE? I KNOW THIS WOULD WORK.
WELL, WE GOT A FEW CREEPS OFF THE STREET, GUESS IT WASN'T **SO** BAD.
I KNOW I'M SUPPOSED TO SAY SOMETHING FANCY, BUT THE TRUTH IS, I NEED TO GET BACK AND DO HOMEWORK.
WE SHOULD DO THIS AGAIN SOMETIME.
IF YOU WANT TO APPLY, I HAVE AN AD ON GREGSLIST SEEKING A NEW SIDEKICK.
THANKS, BUT I'M **NOBODY'S** SIDEKICK.
WEIRDO.
THE END... ...OR IS IT?!?!?!?

META-GIRL

AGE: 21

HOMETOWN:
BURBANK, CA

OCCUPATION:
PHYSICS STUDENT

HISTORY: CHLOE ANDERSON IS YOUR TYPICAL QUIET, NERDY GIRL WHO FOCUSES ON HER STUDIES, AND IT'S PAID OFF WITH HER BECOMING AN AIDE TO PROFESSOR FITCH, A PROMINENT PHYSICIST AND INVENTOR AT THE UNIVERSITY OF SOUTHERN CALIFORNIA. SHE TESTS HIS GADGETS AS HE CREATES THEM, MOST FAMOUSLY HIS ANTI-GRAVITY ELLIPSES, WHICH ALLOW THE POWER OF FLIGHT THROUGH BRAINWAVE CONTROL. RECENTLY, SHE DECIDED TO MOONLIGHT AS THE COSTUMED VIGILANTE, **META-GIRL**. SHE TRIES TO KEEP HER IDENTITY SECRET FROM HER FRIENDS AND FAMILY TO KEEP THEM SAFE AND SO THEY WON'T WORRY, BUT SHE HAS TROUBLE KEEPING HER MULTIPLE LIVES SEPARATED.

PERSONAL LIFE: HER PARENTS **RICHARD** AND **TRISTEN ANDERSON** STILL RESIDE IN BURBANK AND VISIT USC UPON OCCASION. CHLOE IS DATING **JOHNNY BENVINUTI**, A COFFEE SHOP OWNER IN DOWNTOWN L.A. SHE LIVES IN HER APARTMENT WITH HER BEST FRIEND, **HANNAH COMBS**.

JOHNNY BENVINUTI

AGE: 28

HOMETOWN:
LAS VEGAS, NV

OCCUPATION:
COFFEE SHOP OWNER, FENCE

HISTORY:

JOHNNY COMES FROM A NOTORIOUS ORGANIZED CRIME FAMILY, CURRENTLY HEADED BY HIS UNCLE MARCO. HE DOESN'T ENJOY VIOLENCE OR THE PROTECTION RACKET, SO HE'S TRIED TO SETTLING INTO A LESS VIOLENT LIFE AS A FENCE. BUSINESS HAS BEEN BOOMING, SO HE SET UP HIS COFFEE SHOP, **JOHNNY BEANS**, AS A FRONT. HIS BUSINESS HAS BEEN EXPANDING RAPIDLY THANKS TO HIS PRIMARY CLIENT, **PETER BUXTON**, WHO HAS BEEN BRINGING JOHNNY HIGH-PROFILE GOODS AS OF LATE.

PERSONAL LIFE: JOHNNY WASN'T LOOKING FOR LOVE, BUT WHEN **CHLOE ANDERSON** CAME INTO HIS COFFEE SHOP, HE COULDN'T KEEP AWAY FROM HER. THEY'RE CURRENTLY DATING. HE STAYS AWAY FROM HIS IMMEDIATE FAMILY BECAUSE HE DOESN'T WANT TO DELVE TOO DEEPLY INTO THE ORGANIZED CRIME LIFE, BUT THE PRESSURE IS ALWAYS THERE.

HANNAH COMBS

AGE: 21

HOMETOWN:
ORANGE, CA

OCCUPATION:
STUDENT

HISTORY:
HANNAH COMES FROM A WEALTHY FAMILY WHO DONATED HEAVILY TO **USC** BECAUSE OF PAST CONNECTIONS. UNDER IMMENSE PRESSURE TO ATTEND THE SCHOOL, HANNAH SIGNED UP, BUT SHE DOESN'T FIT IN WITH A SERIOUS COLLEGE LIFE. SHE LIKES TO SPEND HER TIME PARTYING, SHOPPING, CLUBBING, EATING AT POSH RESTAURANTS AND HITTING THE GYM. SHE VIEWS LIFE AS SOMETHING TO LIVE AND HAVE FUN, AND DOESN'T WANT TO WASTE HER YOUTH WORKING.

PERSONAL LIFE: HANNAH IS ROOMMATES WITH **CHLOE ANDERSON** AND KNOWS HER ROOMMATE IS **META-GIRL**, EVEN THOUGH CHLOE THINKS SHE'S KEEPING IT A SECRET. SHE'S INTERESTED IN **PAUL**, THE LOCAL BARISTA AT **JOHNNY BEANS**, BUT HE REMAINS ALOOF DESPITE HER SIGNALING HER INTEREST. HER PARENTS ARE GETTING FED UP WITH HER POOR GRADES AND ARE CONSIDERING TAKING AWAY HER APARTMENT AND CREDIT CARD (WHICH THEY PAY FOR).

PAUL HARDY

AGE: 25

HOMETOWN:
INGLEWOOD, CA

OCCUPATION:
BARISTA

HISTORY:
PAUL IS WHAT MANY MIGHT CALL A LATE-BLOOMER. HE MESSED AROUND IN HIGH SCHOOL, GOT POOR GRADES AND NEVER BOTHERED GOING TO COLLEGE. HE SPENT HIS EARLY TWENTIES PARTYING AND PLAYING VIDEO GAMES, BUT NOW HE IS TRYING TO GET HIS LIFE BACK ON TRACK. HE APPLIED FOR THE BARISTA JOB AT **JOHNNY BEANS** AND IMMEDIATELY IMPRESSED THE OWNER, **JOHNNY BENVINUTI.** IT'S BEEN SEVERAL MONTHS, AND PAUL IS BEGINNING TO NOTICE THERE'S A LOT MORE GOING ON AT JOHNNY BEANS THAN JUST SERVING COFFEE. AS AN AMBITIOUS GUY, HE WANTS A PIECE OF THE ACTION.

PERSONAL LIFE: PAUL'S NEVER REALLY HAD A SIGNIFICANT OTHER, AVOIDING THE TOPIC AT FAMILY GATHERINGS WHEN HE BOTHERS TO ATTEND. HIS PARENTS ARE SEPARATED, AND NEVER GAVE HIM MUCH SUPPORT, SO HE DOESN'T FEEL COMPELLED TO SPEND TIME WITH THEM NOW. HE'S THE YOUNGEST OF FOUR BROTHERS, NEVER FEELING LIKE HE QUITE FIT IN AND IS CONTENT TO DO HIS OWN THING.

META-MAN

AGE: 83 (APPEARS 20).

HOMETOWN: SAN DIEGO, CA

OCCUPATION: SPECIAL MILITARY OPERATIONS

HISTORY: DURING THE KOREAN WAR, PILOT **JAMES MILLER** FLEW OVER THE KOREAN PENINSULA ON A BOMBING RUN, ONLY TO CRASH INTO A STRANGE GLOWING SUBSTANCE WHICH FLOATED MID-AIR. HE MANAGED TO EJECT, AND WHEN HE DID, HE FOUND HE HAD OBTAINED MULTIPLE POWERS: FLIGHT, INVULNERABILITY, AND IMMORTALITY. AFTER UNDERGOING SUCH A STRANGE METAMORPHOSIS, HE TOOK THE NAME **META-MAN** AND DEDICATED HIS LIFE TO PROTECTING AMERICA AND THE INNOCENT.

PERSONAL LIFE: JAMES MILLER IS A WIDOWER, WHO WAS MARRIED TO **BETTY**, A NURSE HE MET ON THE MIDWAY AIRBASE DURING THE KOREAN WAR. LITTLE IS KNOWN ABOUT HIS MODERN PERSONAL LIFE, AS HE'S GONE INTO SECLUSION THE LAST HALF CENTURY, SAVE FOR HIS PUBLIC WORK AS META-MAN. HE SEEMS TO HAVE TAKEN AN INTEREST IN MENTORING **META-GIRL**, AND ALLOWS HER TO USE THE SUPERPOWERED "FAMILY" NAME.

BOB BOBINSON

AGE: 32

HOMETOWN:
LAS VEGAS, NV

OCCUPATION:
HENCHMAN

HISTORY:
BOB BOB FIRST GOT HOOKED UP WITH THE BENVINUTI CRIME FAMILY WHEN HE WAS A TEENAGER, WHEN HE WAS A WAITER IN LAS VEGAS, AND DON MARCO BENVINUTI SAW HIS NAMETAG AND THOUGHT "BOB BOBINSON" WAS TOO FUNNY. HE DECIDED TO HAVE THE KID AROUND, AND BOB BECAME A LOYAL FOLLOWER UP UNTIL MARCO'S DEATH. HE NOW SERVES FOR JOHNNY BENVINUTI.

PERSONAL LIFE: BOB IS THE LOS ANGELES MEN'S RECREATIONAL BOWLING LEAGUE ORGANIZER. HE HAS A WIFE BUT TRIES TO KEEP HER AWAY FROM HIS BUSINESS.

MARIO CAPO

AGE: 32

HOMETOWN:
LOS ANGELES, CA

OCCUPATION:
HENCHMAN

HISTORY:
MARIO IS THE TYPE OF GUY PEOPLE COME TO IN CONFIDENCE, AND SO IT WAS WHEN MARCO BENVINUTI TOLD MARIO ABOUT HIS SECRET STASH OF GOLD BURIED IN THE MOJAVE DESERT. EVEN WITH THE OLD MAN MARCO GONE, NO ONE KNOWS ABOUT IT. LOOSE LIPS SINK SHIPS, SO THEY SAY.

PERSONAL LIFE: DOESN'T TALK MUCH ABOUT HIS PERSONAL LIFE EITHER, BUT DON'T MESS WITH HIS BOWLING NIGHT. IT'S THE ONE NIGHT HE LOOKS FORWARD TO.

www.ingramcontent.com/pod-product-compliance
Ingram Content Group UK Ltd.
Pitfield, Milton Keynes, MK11 3LW, UK
UKHW061958290726
14090UKWH00021B/1277